T0115678

THE CURIOUS SOFA

by

Ogdred Weary

DEY ST.
AN IMPRINT OF
WILLIAM MORROW PUBLISHERS

Copyright © 1961 by Edward Gorey
Copyright renewed 1989 by Edward Gorey

All rights reserved. No part of this book may be used or reproduced in any manner whatsoever without written permission except in the case of brief quotations embodied in critical articles and reviews.

For information, address HarperCollins Publishers, 195 Broadway, New York, NY 10007.

Gorey, Edward, 1925–2000
The curious sofa/Ogdred Weary.
p. cm.
ISBN 978-0-15-100307-5
I. Title.
PS3557.0753C87 1997
741.5'973—dc21 97-24678

Printed in Malaysia
24 RRDA 20 19 18

For others

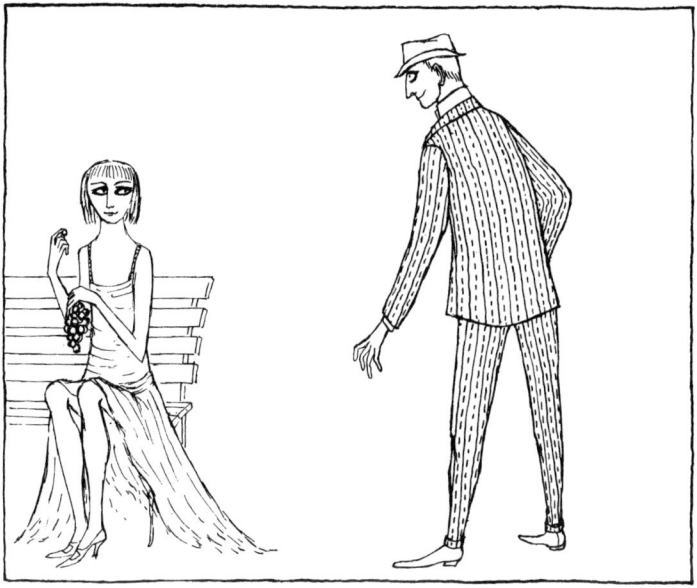

Alice was eating grapes in the park when Herbert, an extremely well-endowed young man, introduced himself to her.

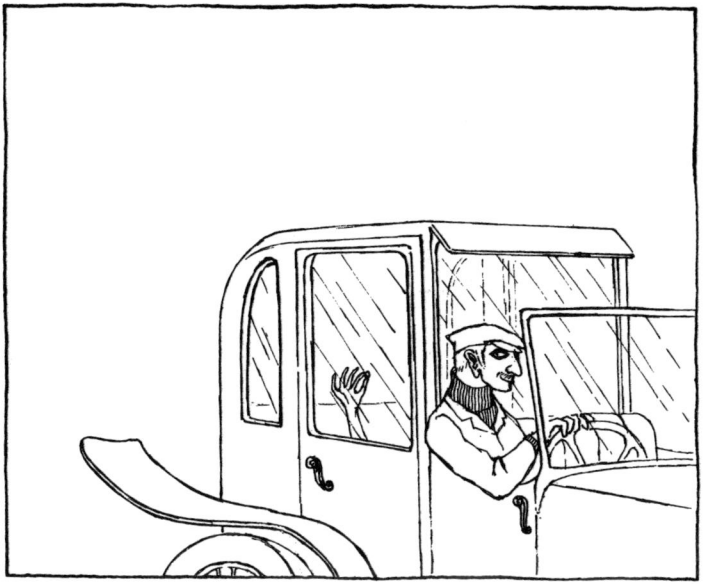

He invited her to go for a ride in a taxi-cab, on the floor of which they did something Alice had never done before.

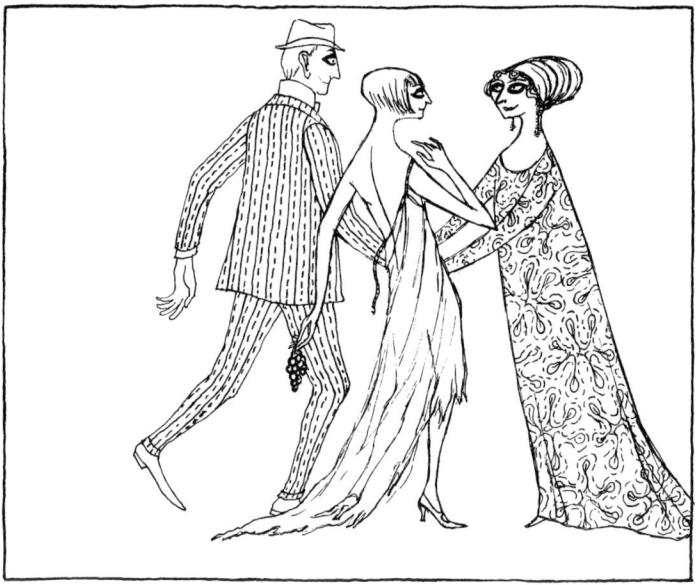

After they had done it several times in different ways, Herbert suggested that Alice tidy up at the home of his aunt, Lady Celia, who welcomed them with great cordiality.

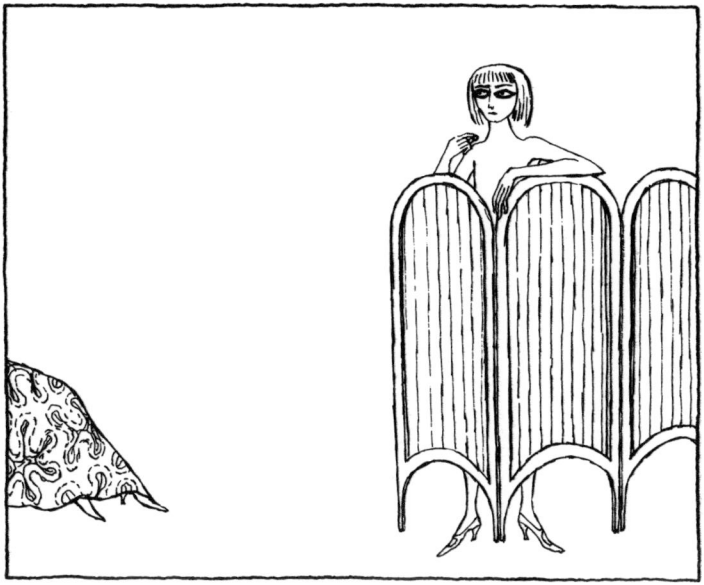

Lady Celia led Alice to her boudoir, where she requested the girl to perform a rather surprising service.

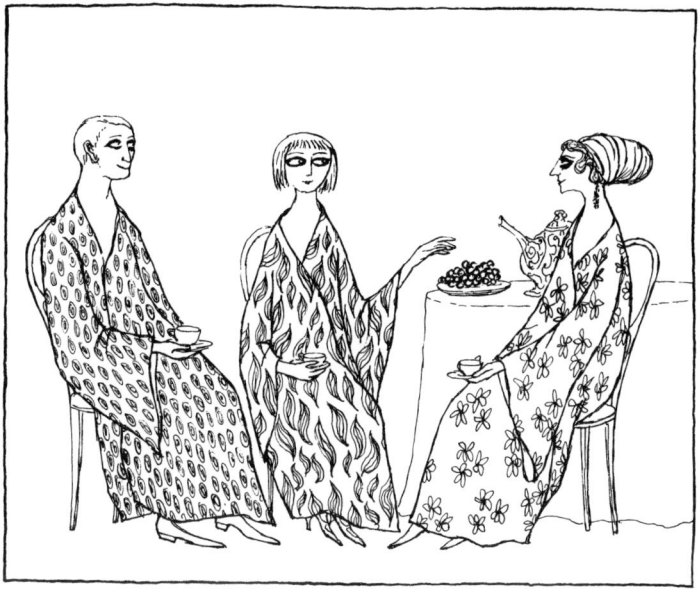

Downstairs the three of them played a most amusing game of Herbert's own invention called "Thumbfumble." They then sat down to a sumptuous tea.

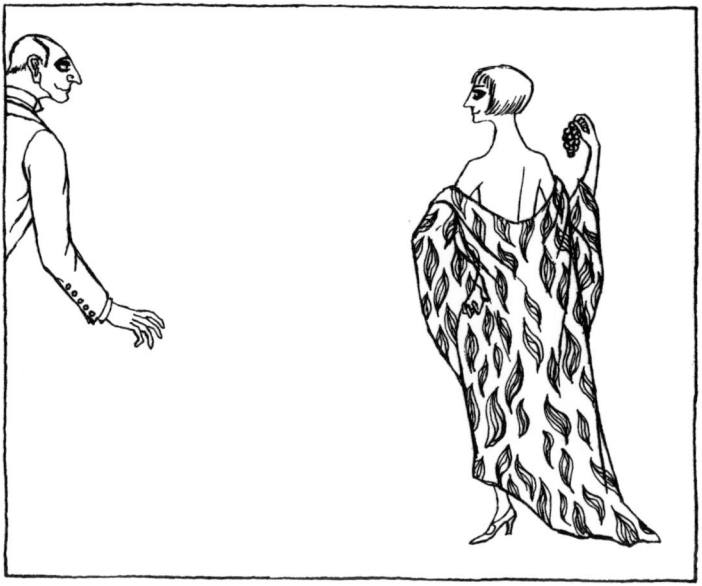

After he had finished the washing-up, Albert, the butler, an unusually well-formed man of middle age, joined them for another frolic. Herbert and Lady Celia had little difficulty in persuading Alice to spend a few days with them.

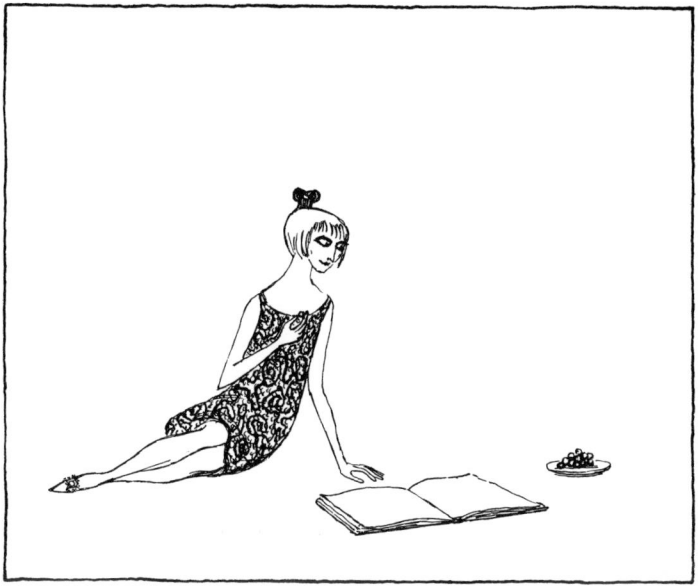

In the interval before dinner she perused an album of instructive chromolithographs entitled ‚Die Sieben und Dreißig Wollüste' which Lady Celia had thoughtfully set out.

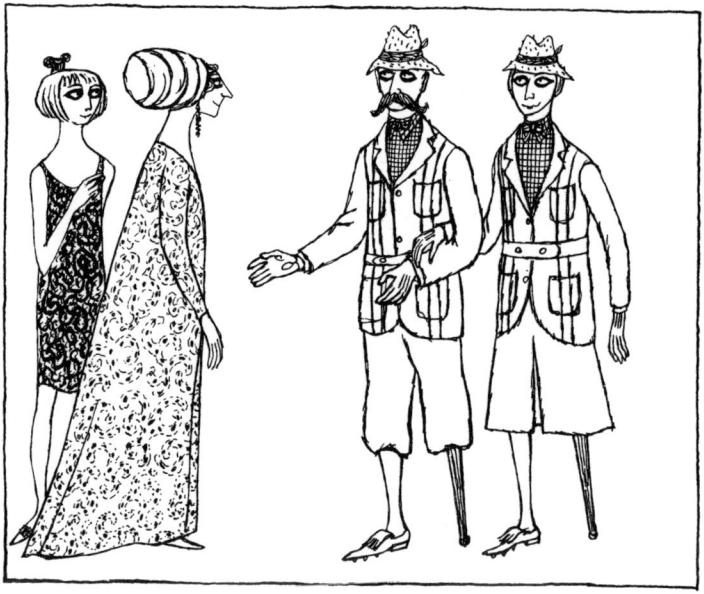

Colonel Gilbert and his wife, Louise, came in after dinner; both of them had wooden legs, with which they could do all sorts of entertaining tricks.

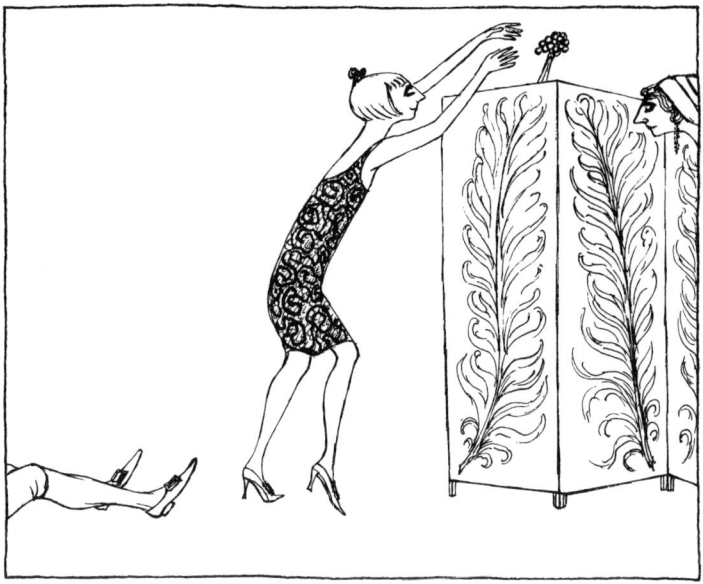

The evening was a huge success, in spite of someone fainting from time to time.

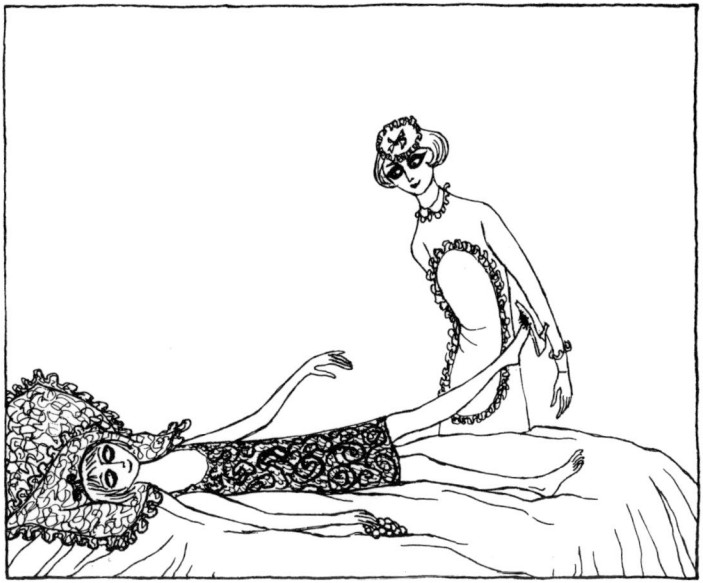

Alice, quite exhausted, was helped to bed by Lady Celia's French maid, Lise, whom she found delightfully sympathetic.

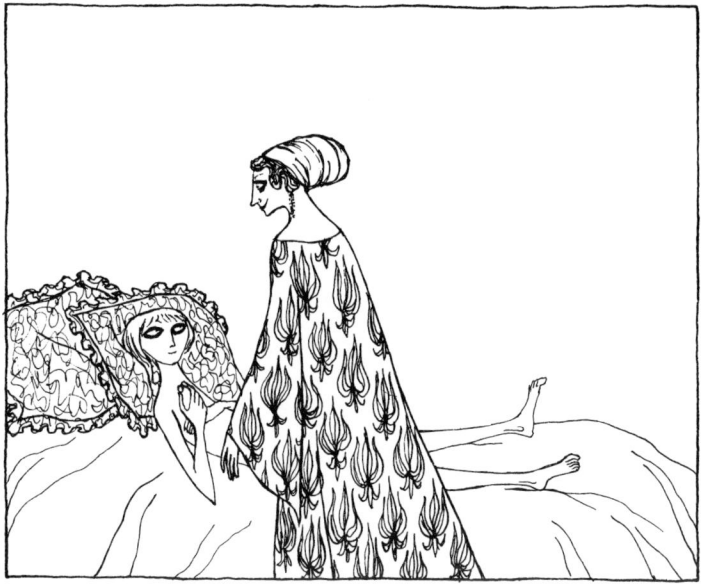

The next morning she was wakened in a novel fashion by Lady Celia in time for elevenses.

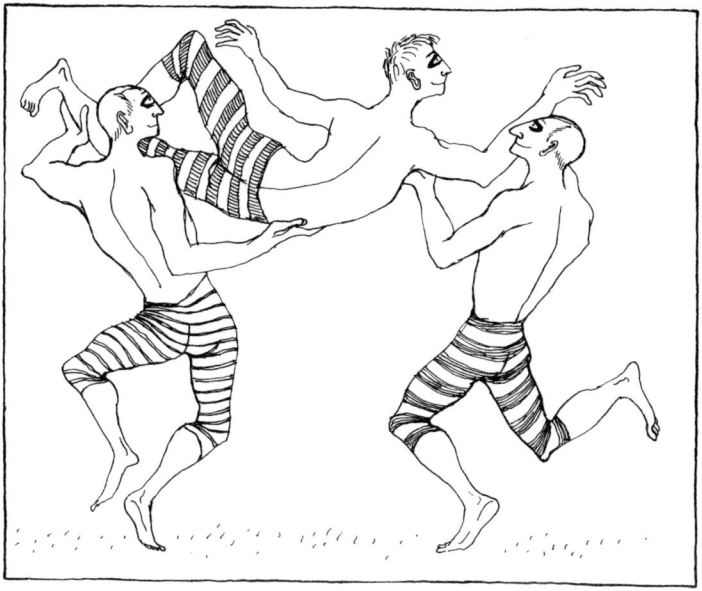

Looking out the window she saw Herbert, Albert, and Harold, the gardener, an exceptionally well-made youth, disporting themselves on the lawn.

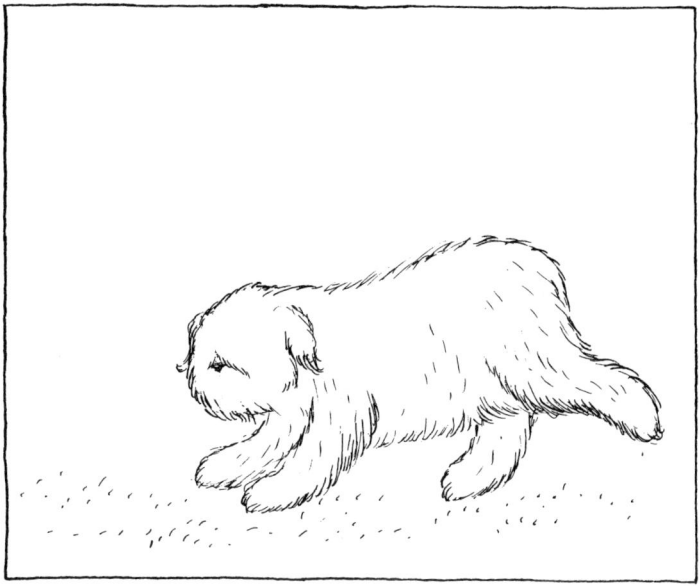

They were soon joined by Donald, Herbert's singularly well-favoured sheepdog, and many were the giggles and barks that came from the shrubbery.

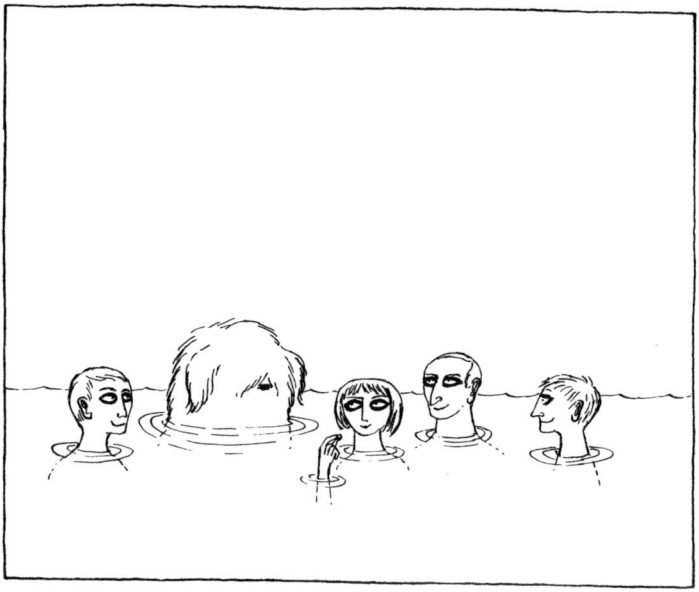

They called up to Alice, who, having put on an ingeniously constructed bathing slip, met them in the pool.

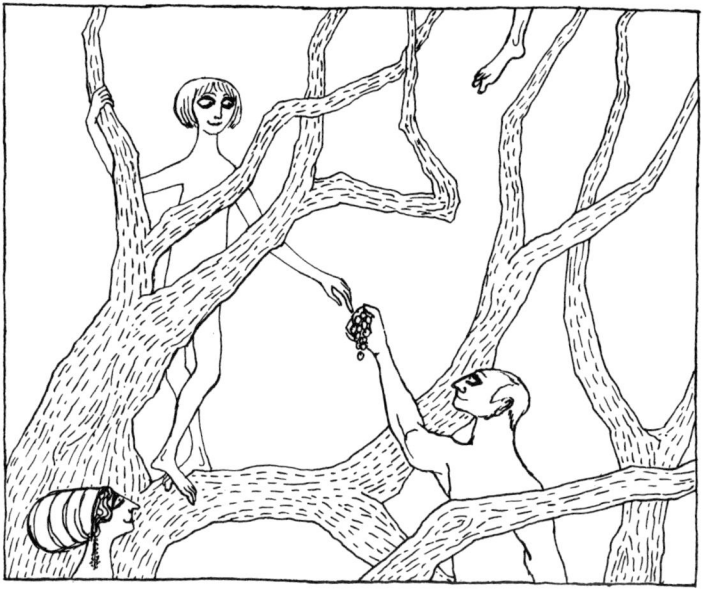

At luncheon, which was alfresco, Lady Celia announced they were invited to the Gilberts for the weekend.

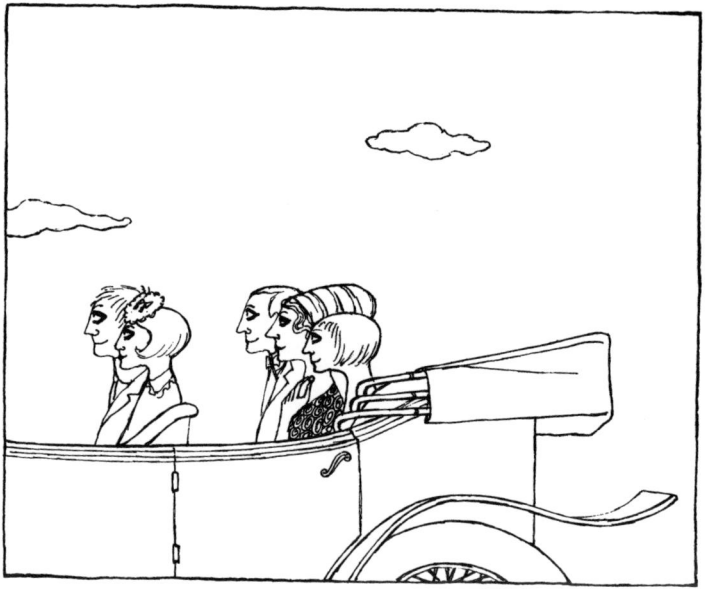

To beguile the tedium of the journey, Albert read aloud from Volume Eleven of the "Encyclopedia of Unimaginable Customs."

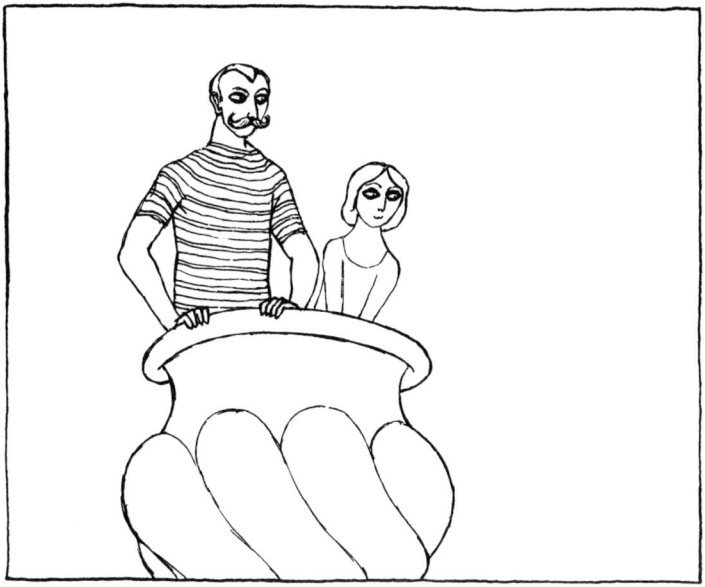

As they drove up to the house, Lucy, the Gilbert's daughter, and Gerald, her fiancé, an uncommonly well-shaped older man, emerged from an ornamental urn.

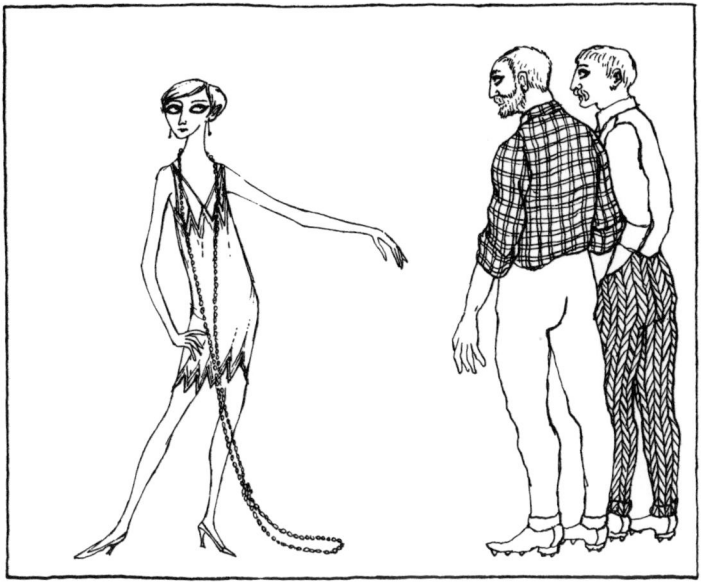

That evening in the library Scylla, one of the guests who had certain anatomical peculiarities, demonstrated the "Lithuanian Typewriter," assisted by Ronald and Robert, two remarkably well-set-up young men from the village.

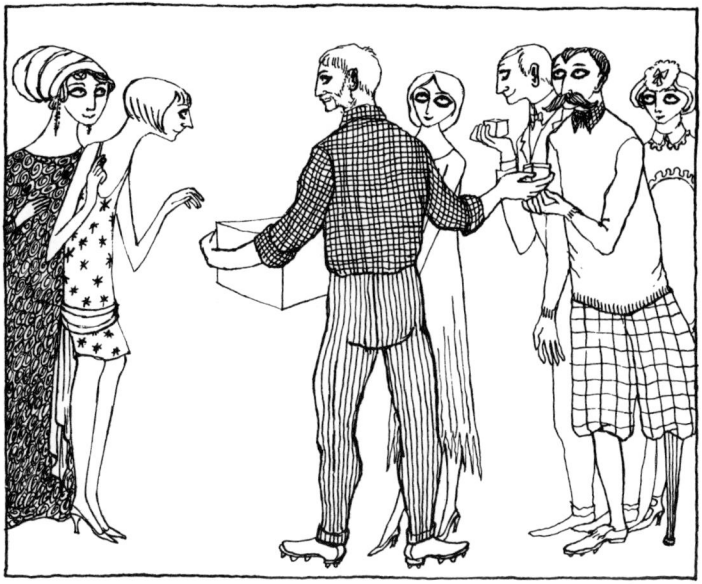

Later Reginald, another remarkably well-set-up young man from the village, provided everyone with the most astonishing little device.

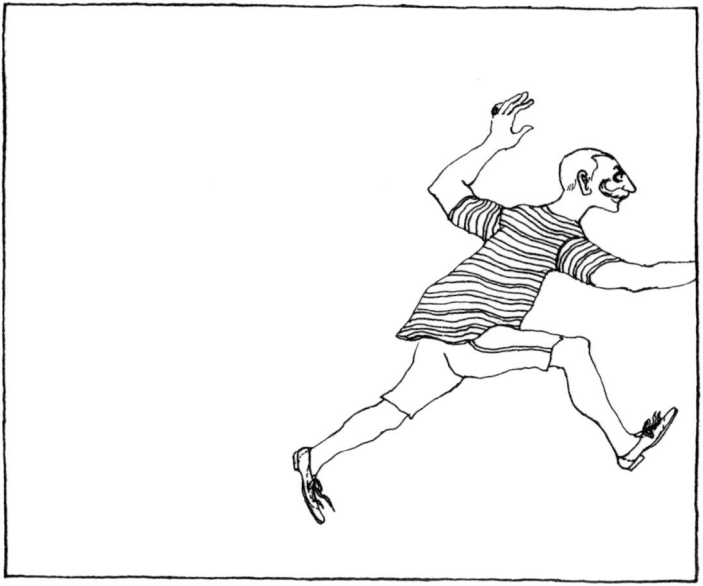

Still later Gerald did a terrible thing to Elsie with a saucepan.

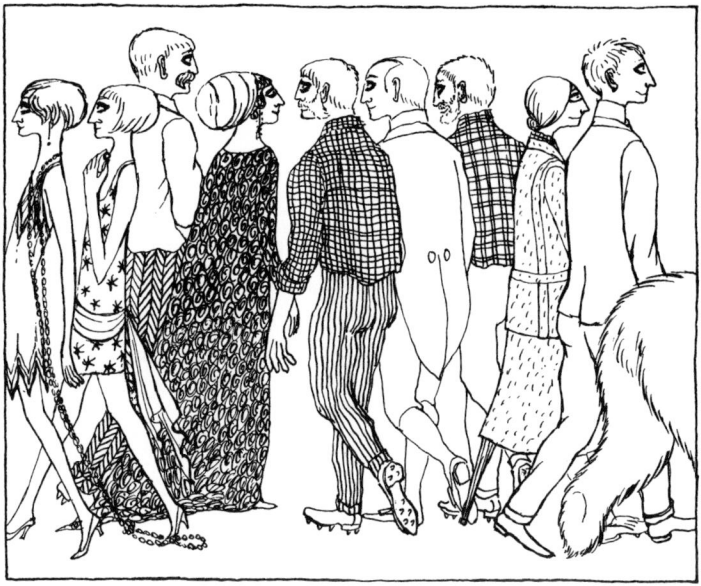

The party split into twos and threes before retiring.

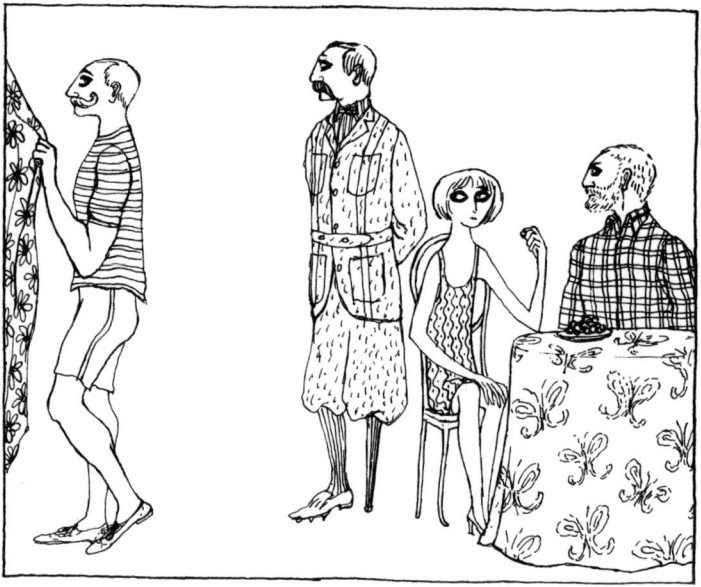

At breakfast it was learned that Elsie had expired during the night, and gloom descended on everybody.

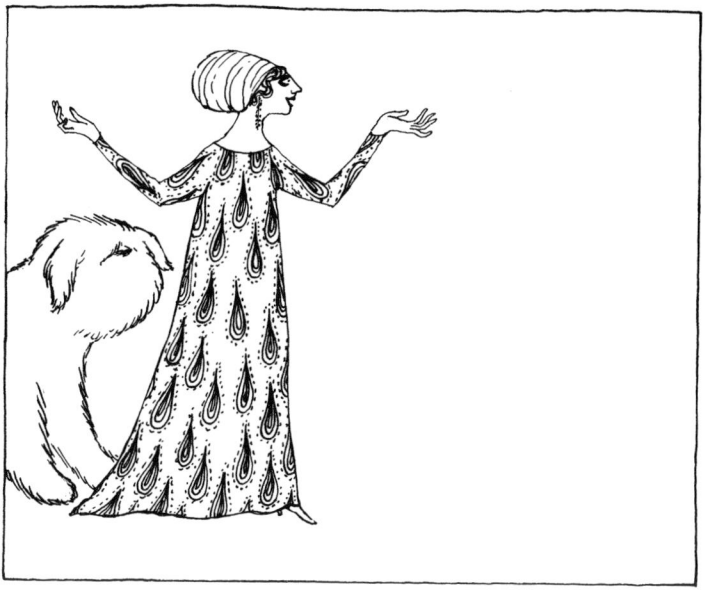

When a change of scene was proposed, Lady Celia suggested a visit to the nearby seat of Sir Egbert, a dear friend of her youth.

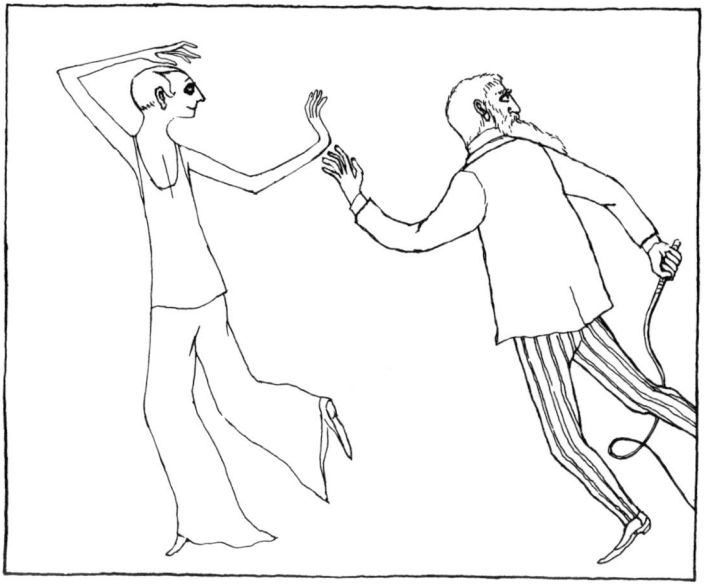

When they got there, they found Sir Egbert, an extraordinarily well-proportioned old gentleman, and his friend, Louie, having a romp on the terrace.

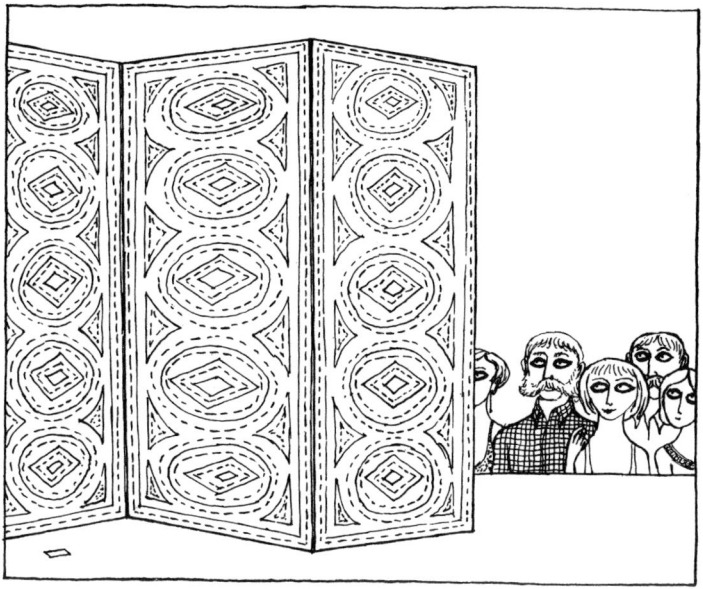

They all went indoors and worked up some most intriguing charades.

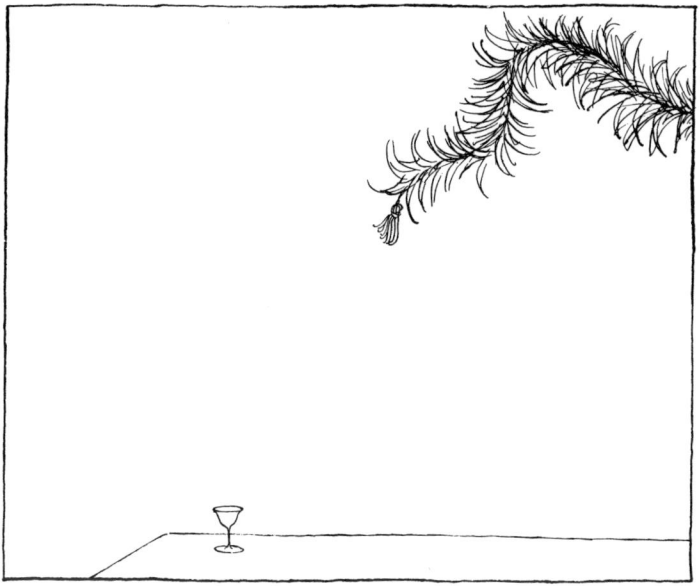

During the light buffet supper
Louie did a dance with a boa.

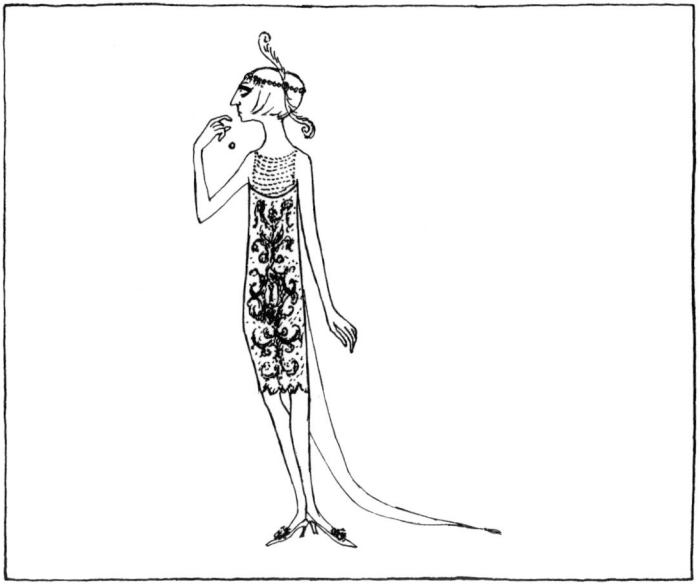

Sir Egbert offered to show them his famous sofa. Alice felt a shudder of nameless apprehension.

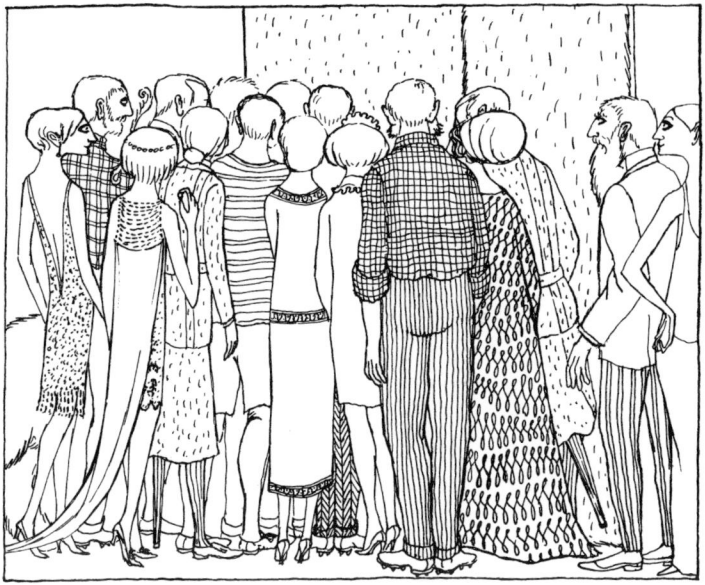

It stood in a windowless room lined with polar bear fur and otherwise empty; it was upholstered in scarlet velvet, and had nine legs and seven arms.

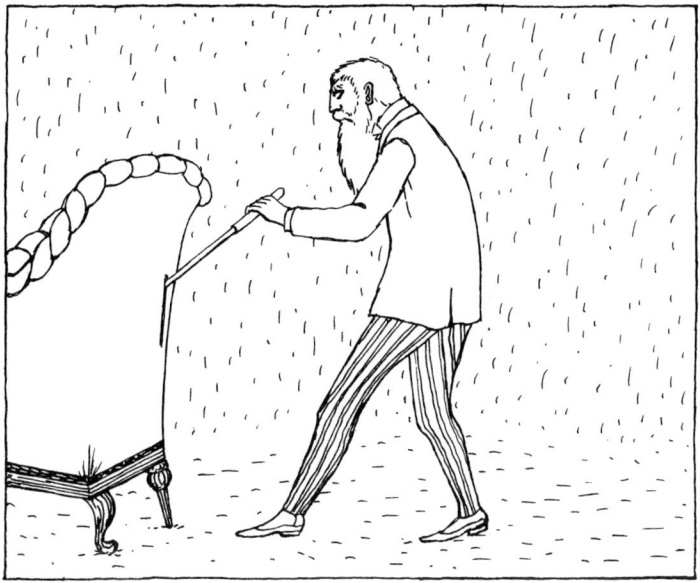

As soon as everybody had crowded into the room, Sir Egbert fastened shut the door, and started up the machinery inside the sofa.

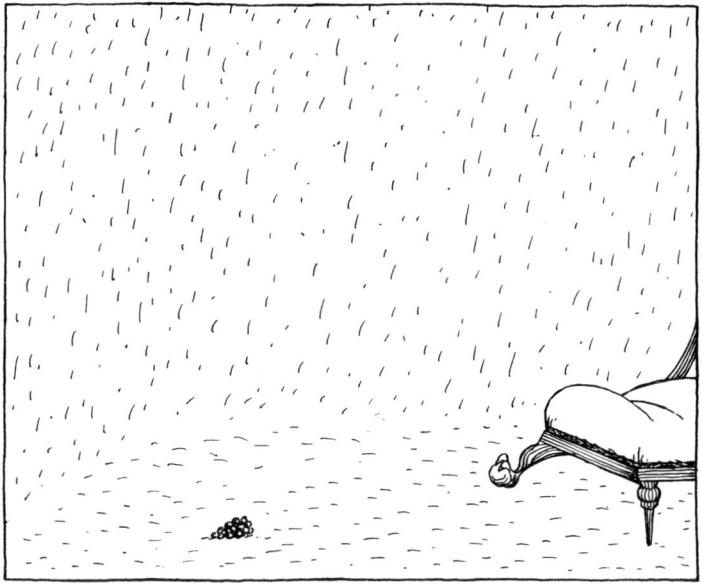

When Alice saw what was about to happen, she began to scream uncontrollably....